The Two Gentlemen of Verona

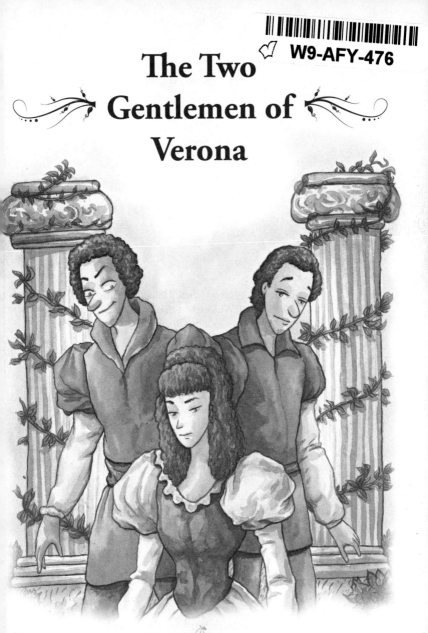

Sweet Cherry
Publishing

Published by Sweet Cherry Publishing Limited
Unit E, Vulcan Business Complex,
Vulcan Road,
Leicester, LE5 3EB,
United Kingdom

First published in the USA in 2013
ISBN: 978-1-78226-079-0

©Macaw Books

Title: The Two Gentlemen of Verona
North American Edition

Text & Illustration by Macaw Books 2013

www.sweetcherrypublishing.com

Printed and bound by Wai Man Book Binding (China) Ltd. Kowloon, H.K.

About *Shakespeare*

William Shakespeare, regarded as the greatest writer in the English language, was born in Stratford-upon-Avon in Warwickshire, England (around April 23, 1564). He was the third of eight children born to John and Mary Shakespeare.

Shakespeare was a poet, playwright, and dramatist. He is often known as England's national poet and the "Bard of Avon." Thirty-eight plays, 154 sonnets, two long narrative poems, and several other poems are attributed to him. Shakespeare's plays have been translated into every major existent language and are performed more often than those of any other playwright.

Proteus: He is a young gentleman from Verona. At the beginning of the play, he is in love with Julia. However, as the play progresses, he falls for Silvia and banishes his best friend, Valentine, from Milan.

Valentine: He is Proteus's best friend and loves Silvia. He becomes leader of the outlaws after he is banished by the duke when Proteus betrays him.

Julia: She is Proteus's beloved. She follows Proteus to Milan, disguised as a page called Sebastian, and does Proteus's bidding.

Silvia: She is the daughter of the Duke of Milan and the beloved of Valentine. She dismisses Proteus's advances, saying that he is doing wrong to Julia. Later, she flees to the forest to avoid marrying Thurio.

The Two Gentlemen of Verona

Valentine and Proteus were two young gentlemen who lived in the city of Verona. They were such good friends that there was hardly a moment they did

not spend together. However, Proteus was in love with a noble and dignified lady called Julia, and when he went to visit her, Valentine would be left all alone. The two friends thought alike on most matters, except of course the subject of love.

"I do not know how you can lose yourself in love like that. Look at yourself, always in a state of anxiety and fear!" Valentine would make fun of Proteus. But even though they never agreed on this topic, the two friends were inseparable.

One day, Valentine came
to Proteus and declared that
he was off to Milan. Proteus
of course did not want to lose
Valentine's company, even if only
for a short while, but Valentine
could not be dissuaded.

Now that his friend was gone, Proteus sat down to write a letter to Julia and handed it to her maid, Lucetta, to be delivered to the lady of his dreams.

Julia was a noble woman, and though she too loved Proteus in every way that he loved her,

she had to keep up the pretense
to show how indifferent she

was to his affections. So when Lucetta gave her the letter, she screamed at her maid for taking letters from Proteus and asked her to leave. However, she was keen to know what her beloved had written and therefore called Lucetta to ask her the time.

Lucetta knew that her lady did not wish to know the time and was interested in the letter, so she once again tried to hand the letter to her. But

Julia was so angry that her maid
knew what was in her heart, that
she immediately tore up the letter
and again asked her to leave.

Once Lucetta was gone,
Julia joined up all the torn bits
of paper and read the letter.
But all she could gather were
a few words here and there.

This upset her and, unable
to contain herself, she wrote
the most endearing letter she
had ever written to Proteus.

Meanwhile,
Proteus's father was
having a discussion
about his son with
a friend. They

were talking about how men
of Proteus's age were either
fighting wars, traveling in
search of new lands or going off
to study in foreign universities,
while all Proteus did was stay at
home. When his father returned
home, he saw that his son was

jumping for joy while reading
a letter. He immediately
asked his son whose letter had
enthralled him so. Proteus
could not tell his father that the
letter was from Julia, who had
reciprocated his love for her.
He said instead, "Oh, it is just

a small matter. It is from Valentine in Milan, and he writes how he has obtained the grace of the Duke of Milan and wishes that I were there with him to be a partner in his fortune."

Hearing this, his father declared, "Even I think that you should indeed join him rather than spending all your time here."

Proteus's father was adamant that his son should leave for Milan immediately and join Valentine. Proteus could find no way out of the lie that he had created and started making preparations for his trip.

Julia was crestfallen that she would have to part with

his company. Both lovers
exchanged vows of love, and
rings, which they would wear
until Proteus returned.

There was, however, a new
development in Milan. Though
Proteus had lied to his father
about Valentine writing to him,
it was in fact true that Valentine

had found the favor of the Duke of Milan and was a regular guest at his court. What no one could have guessed was that Valentine was also in love! He, who used to dissuade his friend Proteus about matters of the heart, was now head over heels in love with

the duke's daughter, Silvia. She too was madly in love with him, but there was a problem. The duke wanted his daughter to be married to a young courtier in his court called Thurio. So the two lovers hid their feelings from the duke for the time being.

One day, as Thurio and Valentine were talking with Silvia, the duke came into his daughter's chambers and told Valentine about the arrival of his friend, Proteus. Valentine was overjoyed to hear about

his friend's visit and praised Proteus. Hearing this, the duke cordially welcomed Proteus and the two friends were reunited.

The moment they were alone together, Valentine lost no time in telling Proteus about all that had happened to him in Milan—and most importantly, about Silvia and how he too had now become a fool in love.

Proteus was truly amazed to hear about the change in his friend. However, from the moment he saw the beautiful Silvia, he also fell in love with her, and was so smitten that he forgot all about his love for Julia and his friendship with Valentine.

Meanwhile, Valentine told Proteus that he and Sylvia were madly in love with each other, but that the duke wanted her to marry Thurio. In confidence, he also told Proteus that on that very night, the lovers had made plans to leave Milan and run away to Mantua. Valentine even

showed Proteus a
rope ladder which
he planned to use
to help Silvia climb
out of her window. Little did
Valentine know of the evil
intentions that were already
lurking in his friend's mind.

Proteus immediately went to the duke and told him of Valentine's plan to run away with his daughter, but only after explaining that it was only because of his duty toward the noble duke, who had offered him such a gracious welcome, that he was betraying his friend.

He also told him about the rope
ladder and that Valentine was
going to conceal it in his cloak.

The duke was rather
pleased with Proteus's honesty.
He assured him that he would

not disclose to Valentine the
identity of his informant,
but would make Valentine
confess to his evil intentions.

That evening, the duke
invited Valentine to court. He
told him that he had fallen in
love with another woman and
asked Valentine for his advice

on how to court her. Valentine, with noble intentions in his heart, at once told him that he should send this woman presents and visit her occasionally.

Soon, he started telling the duke that he should run away with his lover if her father was averse to him, and also informed him how he could make a ladder out of ropes. To this, the duke asked him how he would conceal the ladder, and Valentine declared, "Why, my Lord, you can hide it in your cloak!" Hearing this, the duke pulled off Valentine's cloak to reveal his own ladder. Valentine had been caught in the act, and the duke immediately banished him from Milan.

Meanwhile, in Verona, Julia was having a terrible time without her beloved Proteus. Unable to bear the

separation any longer, she, along with her maid, Lucetta, set off toward Milan. To guard themselves against dangers on the road, both Julia and Lucetta dressed themselves as boys.

On reaching Milan, they went to an inn and took lodgings there. Julia was anxious about how Proteus would look upon

her now that she had shed all her
dignified, ladylike mannerisms
and followed her love to another
city. Seeing her in such a sad
state, the innkeeper asked her to
come and hear some music to
cheer her up. He told her that a
young man was going to play for
his ladylove. Julia readily agreed.

That evening, still dressed as a young boy, she accompanied the innkeeper to listen to the love songs. But to her dismay, she found that they were being sung by Proteus to woo Silvia. Her heart sank. However, there was some respite when Silvia refused his affection, declaring him to be unfaithful to the lady he had left in Verona, as well as to his good friend Valentine.

Though Julia was shocked to see the manner in which

her beloved Proteus was
behaving in Milan, she still
loved him very much. After
some inquiry, she found
out that he was in search
of a servant for himself.
Through the innkeeper, she
managed to get the job—as
Sebastian, the young boy
she was pretending to be.

And so it would be that
Julia, or rather Sebastian, would
be sent to Silvia's chambers with
gifts and letters from Proteus
declaring his love for her. Proteus
also gave her the ring that he and
Julia had exchanged when he left
for Milan. But Julia was fortunate

to hear that Silvia completely
spurned all Proteus's advances.
Soon, the two started talking
about Proteus's love in Verona,
and upon being asked
about her appearance,
Sebastian replied, "Julia
is about my height,

and of my complexion, the color of her eyes and hair are the same as mine." When Sebastian presented her with the ring, Silvia was furious. She said, "How insensitive he is that he sends me the same ring that she had given him. Tell him that I do not accept any of his gifts." These kind words made Julia feel a lot better in her heart.

Poor Valentine was having a rather difficult time. As he was on his way out of Milan, a group of robbers crossed his path and attacked him. But Valentine told them how he had been banished from Milan and all he had were the clothes he wore. The robbers

then said that
they wished him
to be their leader.
Valentine, being at
the rough end of
fate, accepted their
offer. However, he
asked them to show
compassion toward
women and the people
they stole from.

The situation
was getting rather
troublesome for Silvia
at that moment.
Her father was
adamant that she
marry Thurio soon,
and Proteus was

sending her letters and gifts
declaring his love. But all she
could think of was the state
Valentine was in. Unable to
deal with the situation any
longer, she decided to run
away to Mantua, where
she was sure she would be
able to find Valentine.

Along with a noble old
gentleman, Silvia left that

night and headed off toward
Mantua, hopeful that she
would soon be reunited with
Valentine. On the way, she had
to pass through the fearful forest
where Valentine and his group
of robbers were active. As they
entered the forest, Valentine's
robbers took her, while her
escort managed to escape.

Even though they kept
reassuring her that their leader, to
whom they were taking her, was
a noble and virtuous man,
especially toward women,
that was of little
consolation to Silvia.
Suddenly, Proteus
came before them.
He was still attended

by his new servant, Sebastian,
and within minutes he was able
to overpower all the robbers
and managed to save Silvia.

This made Julia rather
worried, as she felt that this act
of Proteus might change Silvia's

feelings toward him. Just as these thoughts were rushing through her head, Valentine emerged. He had heard that his men had abducted a lady, and therefore he had made haste to come to her rescue.

On finally being confronted
by his friend, Proteus felt remorse
and guilt. He broke down before
him and begged for forgiveness.
Valentine, noble soul that he was,
not only forgave him for all that
he had done, but also said, "All
the interest that I have in Silvia, I
give it up to you." Upon hearing

these words, Julia fainted. She felt that Proteus would now once again declare his love for Silvia, and she could perhaps agree.

All of them immediately tried to revive Sebastian. As he came round, he handed over a ring, saying, "I had forgotten, my master ordered me to deliver this ring to Silvia."

But this was the ring that Proteus had given Julia at the time of leaving Verona, and he could not understand how his servant, Sebastian, had got hold

of it. To which Sebastian replied, "Julia herself gave it to me."

It was then that Proteus realized Sebastian was none other than Julia. He was so moved by her love and affection for him that his own feelings of love for her returned.

As the four lovers were expressing their happiness, the Duke and Thurio arrived in search of Silvia. Thurio immediately tried to grab Silvia away from Valentine, to which Valentine replied, "Thurio, keep back. If once again you say that Silvia is yours, you shall embrace your death." Coward that he was, Thurio immediately ran away from the scene.

The Duke now realized what a bad choice the coward

Thurio would have been for his daughter. He immediately embraced Valentine and declared that he had truly won the hand of his daughter.

So, the four lovers soon returned to Verona, where they were married and lived happily ever after.